Addran IV

Ben Winston

Addran IV

Ben Winston

Published by Blue Space Publications, LLC., 2024.

ADDRAN IV

First edition. February 1, 2024.

ISBN: 979-8224952380

Written by Ben Winston.

Also by Ben Winston

Abraxis Complex
Origin of Prometheus
Sword of Damocles
Abraxis Code

Bedouin's Travels
Twilight Earth
The Long, Dark Night
Terra Dawning

Book of the Guardian
Home
Pest Control
The Last Mission
Resolution

Talosian Chronicles
Olympus
Star Dancer
Talosian Alliance
Neptune's Massif
Raptor Squadron
Armageddon

Temple of S.A.R.A.H.
Prototype - Episode I
Subroutines - Episode II
Base Functions - Episode III
Hard Wired
Debug Mode
Beta Test - Episode VI
Upgrades - Episode VII

Tides of Mars
Ascension
Conflict
Tides of Mars (Omnibus Version)

Standalone
Pollux Paradox

Addran IV

Watch for more at bluespace-publications.com.

Table of Contents

Episode One- Inception

The work is dedicated to those few people in our world who help others without questions or reservations, regardless of relation or coercion. They help for no other reason than someone needs it.

Forward

In the latter part of the twenty-first century, man had finally drained their world of natural resources, and so decided it was financially feasible to begin to explore other planets A few planets that were 'local' to Earth had been colonized by large corporations to exploit the resources found there.

When an odd 'wormhole' formed near one of these remote colonies, a probe was sent through to see what was on the other side. Several worlds rich in rare substances were discovered. The first of many planned exploitation colonies was sent. It was immediately lost, and the probe found no trace of it ever arriving in the target sector.

Do to odd instabilities during the colony's transit of the wormhole, it was deemed unstable. No rescue mission was sent, the colony was reported lost, and the wormhole listed as off-limits.

At this time, several colonial rebellions had begun against corporate rule. The Corporation appealed to their puppet planetary government for assistance, and the first interplanetary war started with the deaths of billions sick, starving, corporate slaves.

Lost and misplaced colonies were forgotten in the struggle to survive. During the war, one colony on the very fringe of the galactic arm received a faint somewhat garbled message via subspace. The message was assumed to be an enemy ruse, and was filed as such.

It wouldn't be until centuries after the war, the files were discovered when Imperial Archaeological team explored the ruins of the colony. All the information was returned to the Empire for AI analysis. The missing colony was remembered by an Empire that very much needed the resources it had been sent for.

Faron looked out over the desolate plain that was the fractured desert. A place that got so hot, the sand turned to pseudo-glass. Simply setting foot out there without a hard suit was death; a very, very painful death.

As he watched the dust devils blow tiny shards of glass in every direction, he remembered the lessons he'd had to sit through. How humans ended up here, and why. As well as exactly where they now found themselves.

Long ago, A human colony mission departed Sol space for a system on the far side of the galaxy. A 'Super Earth' type planet that was rich with plant life and abundant resources for sustaining life. Addran IV was a garden of Eden and a godsend for the critically overcrowded Sol system. So a colony ship was built, crewed, and stuffed with everything the five thousand new colonists would need to get started. The probes sent to the new planet passed through a transit lane to get to the far side of the galaxy; it was faster than using current faster than light propulsion technology.

Addran IV was found to be closer to the terminus of a different transit lane so when the colony ship set out, they plotted a course using the new transit point. The engineers and astrophysicists believe the lane bisected a black hole. This was undoubtedly the planet they had been trying to reach, but many, many years in the future. They believed that sometime between the time the ship left Sol, and arrived at Addran, a good-sized comet had collided with one of the two primary stars causing it to become a flare star.

The fourth planet was now a desolate desert world with scarce water and even scarcer fauna. What native creatures were left on the surface, were very hostile, and very aggressive. Once the ship crash-landed on the planet, the crew attempted to send a message back to Earth to request help. The only reply was static.

Whether through war or natural phenomena, communications with Sol had never been established after planet-fall. The fate of the home system was unknown.

Water was quickly located; deep underground or in massive cisterns deep in the mountains. Food was grown mostly in the polar regions, away from the worst effects of the solar flare's effects. Mineral mining, processing, and manufacturing were scattered all over the planet.

That was all a long time ago in Faron's view. His revere was broken as a hover train decelerated out in the desert. The sonic disturbance was not audible inside the underground city, but out here, on the sheltered veranda, he could hear it even though it was almost a hundred kilometers away. Out there, in the blasted sand, the thunderous boom was proceeded by many small, bright flashes from the crushed pseudo-glass.

He smiled at the sight; very soon, he would be driving one of the big trains himself. He'd been training most of his life for the job. A train engine was a cold fusion-powered, electromagnetic, super-sonic missile that carried massive amounts of cargo and passengers all over a very large planet.

Today he was to meet his navigator. The big trains were run by a mated couple (or more, for specialty trips) that relied on each other as they shared the duty and responsibility of their assigned vocation.

Faron was a very bright young man. He would be graduating to adulthood later this month when all the other young people in his class passed the final rite of childhood. The final tests in training and the evaluations of his instructors are what would determine if he was to be judged as an adult.

He turned and walked for the door back into the hidden city. As he walked, he thought about what he faced. Biologically, he and the others in the class were in their early twenties. The slower rotation of Addran made their local age fifteen. The Rite of Service marked the class' sixteenth day of birth, and they became officially adults.

Faron had never heard of anyone failing the Rite and not advancing, so he believed it was simply one of the things the Elders liked to attend and give endless speeches at. As he entered the academy level, he began seeing others of his class. But this time, mixed in with the other boys, were groups of girls from the other side 0f the academy. He'd seen and spoken to some of the girls before, but normally the two classes were kept separate. Faron knew that would end today as teams were assigned. He secretly hoped his new wife would be a nice person.

He'd heard a rumor that after their last meeting, the girls were told who their new mate would be. They were given a data stack of their selected mate so they could make the final decision to accept the matching. None of the boys knew if they had been rejected or traded to someone else.

For the boys, they had until the Rite of Service to decide if the pairing was acceptable. After that, it became permanent. When this meeting with his instructor ended, he would meet his new mate at their new quarters. Domestic drones were actually moving all personal belongings during the meetings.

Not everyone was a pilot candidate. All the 'children' had studied different and differing fields. However, they would be meeting their assigned mate today as well.

The man at the door smiled at him as he approached. He had been Faron's Engineering instructor. "Faron Basie, welcome. Before I tell you your new assignment, are you sure I can't talk you into switching to engineering? You could work there while you advanced your knowledge at the Elder Collage!"

"Thank you, Terax, but I've got my heart set on driving. I got hooked in the simulators, and now I can't wait for the real thing!" Faron replied.

The man called Terax nodded his head as he accessed his hand unit. "I figured as much, but I thought I'd at least ask before you left." His unit beeped at him, and he frowned. "Now that's just odd," He looked up at his favorite student. "Uh, you need to report to admin twenty-three. They will give you your new assignment there."

Faron looked back in confusion. "I didn't fail did I?"

Terax shook his head. "No, we had two failures this cycle, and you weren't one of them. I have no idea what's going on."

Faron nodded. "I thought we only had fifteen admins?"

Terax nodded. "We do. Admin twenty-three is command level, near the main engineering hanger. You best not keep whoever called you there waiting. Off with you now, and good speed driver."

"I hope to see you again," Faron said as he turned away. "You were my favorite instructor."

Terax just smiled and nodded to his former student, making shooing motions with his hands.

The engineering hanger was where new trains and other ground vehicles were developed. It was also a long way from the admin section of the academy. Why he was being called down there was a complete mystery to him. He was trained that, mysteries, more often than not, were bad things. When he finally arrived at the designated room, he saw it was labeled as 'Conference Room CS-23-e'. With some trepidation, he took a deep breath and opened the door.

He was surprised to find not one elder but three, as well as four girls from the academy chatting with the Elders. "My apologies for keeping you waiting, Elders."

"Nonsense Captain, you got here precisely on time." The standing man replied. "Just as you should."

"Please, Take a seat with the ladies so we can begin." He gestured to the pretty quintet. With a shock, Faron saw that all four women wore his mate's design on their armbands. These *four* women were his mates, and he'd never met any of them.

Due to the heat on Addran typical clothing was usually a skirt or shorts and soft shoes in the city. Outside the cities, there was a version of the shoe that was designed to protect the foot much better. No one wore top clothing as it was simply too hot for ancient, outdated, modesties. Since no one wore a top, the armband was developed to carry identifying marks and codes.

As he joined them a very pretty blond with dark skin and bright almost glowing blue eyes stepped forward. "Captain, We have selected you. We have been a group since primary instruction. The decision was very unanimous. We should do well together. I am Crista," She finished.

"Jana," said the brunette to her right.

"Janb," said the next girl to the right; she was almost identical to Jana.

"Helna" the girl on the left said, grinning at him.

He could feel that all four young women were completely committed to the group, including him. He nodded to all of them in greeting when they introduced themselves—finally got to one knee before them.

"I am Faron Basie. I am humbled and honored to be selected as your mate. I will never betray the trust you put in me, nor will ever hurt you, our bond, or our children. I will trust in your decision and accept all of you as mates as well," Faron replied and held out his hand between Crista and Jana.

The four smiling women took his offered hand and pulled him to his feet so they could take turns hugging him and kissing his cheek.

The Elder cleared his throat. "I'm sorry to interrupt, but you can carry on getting to know each other in a few minutes. We really must impart to you the significance of your new situation."

Faron, still holding hands with Jana and Crista, and smiling like an idiot, bowed to the Elders. "Our apologies, Elders."

The Elder on the left snorted. "Nonsense! You're excited, and rightly so! It is we who should beg your forgiveness for interfering at such a time."

"Very true, Aitkin," the right Elder said. "Captain, your family will not be receiving a quarters assignment at this time. Instead, your items have been moved into your new train." He looked over to his fellows. "I am Elder Pol, and Elder Aitkin is the one on the far side.

"Elder Bollum will act as your main sponsor here in command. As Aitkin and I only wanted to meet you all, we will leave you now so Bollum can get to it."

After the two Elders left, Elder Bollum smiled at the group. "Based on your performance during instruction, as well as the unusually high compatibility between all of you, the Council has selected you for a very special assignment.

"As of now, everything you learn can only be discussed between the five of you, and myself. No one else can know your true mission. Publicly, you will be driving our newest, and largest sand train. In reality, you will be responsible for the first armed and armored heavy transport," Bollum explained.

Faron lost his grin. "Armed, sir? Why would we need weapons?"

"Please, all of you sit down," the Elder began. "We've begun receiving comm signals from Earth... *Subspace* comm signals."

"Excuse me, Elder, our distress calls went out centuries ago. Why are they only now replying?" Helna asked.

Faron shook his head. "No, there would be no need to arm ourselves for that. Something has changed. Even though the signal was subspace, it couldn't have been been current, or even directed at us."

"Right on both counts," Bollum replied, nodding. "We've overheard enough to want to take some precautions for our continued survival. You five young people are the beginnings of that.

"Out in hanger eighteen, is your new home. The Engine is the length of three regular engines and has three levels. You kids will be living in there for a while, so we made it as comfortable as we could manage. Because of her size, you won't be able to dock at the normal stations, which is actually fine, because your going to be hauling a massive amount of cargo directly to and from the factories or refineries. You will also have five-passenger liners in order to bring in the people we're going to need for this. They will always meet you at the loading areas. You also currently have ten cargo cars, but we plan on adding at least ten more. All cars are triple height and twice normal length," Bollum explained.

"All areas are accessible internally so repairs can be made on the fly. You have the very latest shielding and should be able to run through a flare, but I don't think I'd want to be the one to test it."

"Sir, you said we'd be living in there a while; won't we be staying there?" Janb asked.

Bollum grinned. "We were right, you kids are too smart for us!" he chuckled. "You'll be living on the train for the first twenty years or so, but after that you'll move temporarily to apartments near the engineering section of the moon base. At least until the design for your ship is finished, then you'll be moving aboard that."

"With respect honored Elder. I think perhaps you should tell us exactly what this project is going to entail, that way we can be prepared for our parts of it," Faron said. His concern was clear on his face. "From the sound of it, we're going to be moving a considerable amount of weight."

"And people," Jana added.

Bollum nodded his head. "You are correct, in fact, you'll be moving everything needed to build a new space facility. First you'll move the raw ores to the processing stations, then the processed ore to the manufacturing factories, then the manufactured pieces to the location of the new facility. In addition to that, you'll be hauling the construction crews and their equipment out to the site.

"It sounds like we're going to be busy, husband," Crista said looking at Faron.

"Very true," Faron agreed.

"Now, here is where you're going to have a lot of questions. Once you finish the space facility, we will have also finished a very special upgrade for your train. You will have the ability to haul material and equipment into orbit as well as the moons," Bollum finished, sounding perfectly reasonable.

"We'll be what?" Faron asked in disbelief.

"Holy crap! Look at this thing!" Crista said as the new family walked across the boarding bridge.

"It's going to take me a year of study just to understand the power systems on this monster!" Helna added

"Relax ladies; I'm sure it's not all that different from a normal train," Faron said. "It can't be. Otherwise, how would Crista and I be able to drive it?"

"Besides Helna; we were told not to worry about anything until after we all got to know each other better," Jana said, grinning at her. "Well, for Faron to get to know us anyway."

"I'm looking forward to it," Faron admitted.

"You might want to rethink that, husband," Janb said in her soft voice. "I think your physical endurance will be put to the test this rest period."

The rest of the girls chuckled but agreed.

"So, we're going to have to feed you a lot of proteins to keep your strength up!" Crista said.

"As completely attractive as all of you are, I think you'll be lucky if you make it to dinner time!" Faron replied, grinning evilly.

Crista and Jana pushed their shorts down and off. While Helna and Janb unhooked the wraps they had been wearing, letting them drop to the deck.

"Anytime, anywhere, any of us, Faron," Crista said, seriously. "I would recommend going inside before the crowd behind us gets a real show, though."

"I'm okay with that!" Helna said.

"Helna, you're scary sometimes!" Jana said. "I almost believe you mean that!

"Come on Girls, we can get busy christening the train as soon as we get inside," Crista said in a slightly commanding tone. She was Faron's second and had the same training he'd had.

As he opened the doors for the girls, he looked at Crista. "Why didn't you opt for pilot?"

She shrugged. "Didn't want it really. I think I picked the right place for me. All of the respect, but none of the responsibility."

"Failed the 'crush' test?" Faron asked, ruefully. He was referring to one of the tests given during training. The pilot candidate is taken out on a real train as a pilot, with the real pilot instructor as second. It was the instructor's job to back up the trainee, but to also create scenarios that would test the trainee in crisis.

Faron failed the first scenario but refused to give up. He passed the rest of the test and moved on. However, this test was the most difficult and culled a lot of potential pilots.

"Yes, but it was intentional," Crista replied. "My Instructor was aware of my desire and helped me to create a believable failure. Although I'm sure I would have failed that portion anyway."

Faron nodded. "I did fail one of the scenes. Has a sandstorm ever actually happened during a flare?"

Crista shook her head. "No, never. Theoretically, it could happen, maybe out on the great desert, but no one has ever recorded seeing one." Grinning, she took his hand and pulled him through the hatch.

"Incidentally, that was the test I failed." She gestured to the hatch, "I'd recommend locking that and dropping the sarong. The girls have been looking forward to tonight for a while. I'll help as much as I can, but you're the main attraction."

"Elder Bollum," Faron said over the comm. "Forgive me, but we couldn't help but notice that you're expanding the construction bay we're in. May I ask if you are planning more super trains like this one?"

"You may," Bollum replied. "You're as deep into this project as the rest of us. Yes, we are expanding our construction dock to make room for two more bays the size of the one you're currently in. The plan is to eventually replace as many of our current fleet as we can.

"However, the bay you're in, as well as the train took the better part of two years to get built, and we started with the existing bay. Once we get the bays built, and the next three trains started, we'll swap the standard construction and maintenance station for this one, and begin to upgrade that one. Provided time permits."

"I haven't seen the whole extent of this facility, Sir, but looks like it goes back quite a distance," Faron said. "Is that the reason it takes so long?"

"It is, however, in fairness. The tunnel bay you are in does stretch through the mountains to the great desert on the far side. We won't have to tunnel that much for the new bays. That's called the Deep Sand entrance by the way."

"As to the reason I called, Elder. The ladies tell me they'll be ready to go in three days. As for myself and Crista, we could leave anytime," Faron said.

"Did the other three tell you why they wanted another three days, I'd have thought a week would have been enough," Bollum asked.

"Helna feels she needs to fully understand the navigation suite before we launch, and the other two are inspecting every car. I tried to tell them they had already passed the main inspection, and Helna could learn the flight navs later, but they seem pretty adamant."

Bollum nodded. "I understand. I salute their dedication, but we need to get you moving; they can inspect en route to your first stop. You're correct; Helna can study the new systems in transit. However, before you depart, the medical officer and I would like a word with you. I will also bring your first assignment with me. Please have your crew assembled in your lounge area after the noon meal tomorrow. You will depart after supper."

"It will be done Elder," Faron replied and bowed his head to the screen.

"See you then, son," Bollum said and smiling, closed the channel.

"Before we begin, I'd like to reassure the three of you," Bollum said to the two engineers and the navigator. "This entire train spent the better part of four months being inspected and certified by four Master Engineers and two Elder Engineers. Your mission is so important that no one is willing to take risks. I applaud your dedication in wanting to inspect every inch of this completely new piece of equipment, but the truth is, we don't have the time. You must leave later this day."

"We understand, Elder." The twins replied in unison, causing Bollum to chuckle and shake his head.

He turned to Helna. "Navigator. The computer system installed on this ship is the most advanced we've ever developed and is on par with the Artificial Intelligence in the original colony ship. She will teach you all you need to know by the time you need to know it. I'm certain you'll have plenty of time."

Helna bowed her head to the Elder. "As you say, Elder."

Bollum cleared his throat and addressed everyone. "Now, the reason I've called all of you together is to introduce Elder Gracen. She is a Bio-mechanical Engineer, medical doctor, and surgeon." He nodded to the other Elder as he sat down.

The very young-looking female Elder stood. "What I am about to tell you is extremely secret as well as very important." She looked a little uncomfortable. "A few years ago, a medical procedure was performed on the five of you in preparation for this mission."

"Excuse me, Elder," Faron said. "We just learned of this mission a few days ago. Are you saying we were already preselected?"

"All five of you were selected at the beginning of this project, ten years ago. Yes, you really did have the freedom to pick your own path, although none of you actually did," Bollum replied.

Gracen smiled sadly. "Once your bodies finished maturing, we brought you into the medical area. If you remember we told you it was a final medical test for your future duties."

When all five nodded, she continued. "It was not for a medical test, but instead we performed a medical procedure that transferred you're conscious mind into an android body. That was roughly six years ago, and none of you have figured it out, so we are disclosing it."

"I don't feel like a robot," Crista said softly.

Gracen smiled at her. "Because you're not. You are a bio-mechanical android that has the same needs to function properly as your original human bodies."

"Uh, so what happened to our real bodies?" Faron asked.

"After extracting genetic material for the production of offspring, you were all placed in cryostasis. However, your minds are still linked to your bodies," Gracen explained. "In all the ways that matter, you are experiencing everything you are doing. As an example, none of you even knew of the change. You still feel everything you always did, and if you ever have to revert to your natural bodies, you'll still remember everything just as if it had happened to you."

"So why are you only telling us this now?" Helna asked.

"Because of the very dangerous situation we're putting you in," Bollum answered instead of Gracen. " There are very few people that this procedure has been done for; people that have been deemed important to the survival of the colony as a whole. Because of your training, and the experience you're going to be getting, you are now considered to be a part of that group."

Gracen nodded her head in agreement. "While the Elder council is aware of this, not all of them have been given this procedure. Only you and the original colonists are 'riding' artificial bodies so far. The colonists because our natural bodies could not adjust to this environment." Gracen smiled. "Before you ask, yes; I'm one of the original colonists."

"I, uh, I hope you don't mind, but I'm a little..." Faron hesitated. "This is going to take some thought. May we comm you later if we have questions?"

"Certainly, although, I'll be riding with you for a bit," Gracen replied. "My gear is being loaded into a passenger car as we speak."

Faron nodded and looked at Bollum. "Sir, about our mission?"

Bollum nodded and handed Faron a data stick. "The details are on here, but basically, you'll be taking a tour of the planet as a shakedown. You'll be away from here for about six months unless something changes, and it very well could.

"Your first stop will be the Sundune plateau for raw ores. Also, make sure that Gracen has ample time to perform her mission as well. I'll leave it to her to fill you in on that."

"Elder, given the design and mission of this train, would stealth be a consideration?" Jana asked.

Bollum nodded. "Very much so, we have included the latest in electronic countermeasures we have in the design. You won't be invisible, but you'll be very hard to detect with sensors."

"What if we could be optically invisible as well?" Jana asked.

"You're talking about Celia's pet project?" Janb asked.

Jana nodded to her twin. "She was working on a side project in art class. I tried to tell her to bring it to the instructor's attention, but she kept saying it wasn't important enough to waste her time."

"May I ask what it was she was working on exactly?" Bollum asked.

Jana nodded. "She was trying to perfect a coating that would mimic the stealth ability of a sand raptor. She thought it could add a very beautiful and unique tone to paintings and sculptures. The last time I saw it, she was frustrated because it made her test object completely invisible, instead of partially."

Bollum held up his wrist unit. "Thera?"

"Yes Elder?" a woman answered.

"Locate Celia from the latest class and have her meet me in school admin three in an hour, please."

"Working, Elder. Do you wish to share dinner with her?" Bollum's aide asked.

Bollum smiled and shook his head. "Still mothering me, Thera? Dinner is fine, nothing too fancy, but please make it enjoyable."

"Very good, Elder. I'll make sure it's waiting for the both of you," the woman replied, haughtily.

Bollum chuckled. "No matter how old a person gets, there is still someone trying to mother them."

"Let's wake her up; switch all power systems to internal," Faron ordered.

Jana was typing in commands on her terminal and Crista was watching hers; she nodded. "Power systems are online and report all green. Disconnecting from shore power."

"All aboard if you please, Crista," Faron asked.

"All passengers are accounted for and gangways are clear. Retracting boarding ramps," Crista reported.

"Setting height to four meters for departure; how does our topside clearance look?" Faron asked.

"At least ten more meters, but the doors are lower," Crista said. "I don't think I'd go much higher."

Faron nodded in agreement. "I thought so, keep an eye on it please; with all the equipment we have on top of this lady, I'd hate to rip something off as we're pulling out."

"Especially with our last two cars being full of HCH fuel for our first two stops," Helna mumbled just loud enough to be heard.

"Just wait, Helna. Our next load out of here is probably going to be all fuel," Crista replied, making Helna look a little sick.

"Crista quit tormenting Helna and make a note for Elder Bollum to either raise the portal threshold or program a height restriction into the computer for the trains," Faron replied grinning and shaking his head at the two girls.

"Yes sir," Crista replied. "We're clear of all moorings."

"Thank you, moving us out dead slow," Faron said, as he took the controls and got the big train moving.

"Message from Elder Bollum; 'Suggestions received and appreciated. It will be implemented before you return. Safe journey everyone.' Message ends," Crista said.

"We are exiting port, hull temperature rising to external temperatures," Crista reported.

"Jana, environment systems?" Faron asked.

"Online sir, I'm sure we'd feel it if they weren't" Jana replied. "Ambient temperature is one-thirty-five!"

Faron nodded. "I'll remember to ask next time. Thank you for making sure I don't mess up."

She smiled at him and nodded in reply as Crista spoke. "We will be clear of the port in two minutes, the engine is over open sand."

"Increasing speed to point one," Faron said. "Helna, please set up a course to Cerberus Pass."

Helna nodded. "Course set, Captain. Come left forty-one degrees once clear of the port. Increase speed to one point three for forty-nine hours. Cerberus beacon is set."

"Port control to one-niner-three super heavy. You are clear of Midgard port and free to navigate. Good speed and safe journey,"

"One-niner-three. Understood Control. Thank you; see you in a few months. Super heavy has left the building," Faron said as he started his first turn. "Ride height now at ten meters, Increasing speed to one point three on the Cerberus beacon. Autopilot is now engaged." Releasing the controls, Faron leaned back and looked around. "So, who's turn to cook tonight?"

"I remember the Elder telling us that this train was equipped with the latest AI system. So why doesn't it seem to be working?" Crista asked.

Janb looked a little uncomfortable. "I took her offline for the time being. There is a problem with her interface systems that could cause long-term damage to her personality programming. I might need help from either you or Faron to finish repairs."

"Can't I help you?" Jana asked.

Janb looked at her sister apologetically. "Not with this part, I have to go into her core program, which requires either Faron or Crista to access it. Then too, they've had more training in this type of programming than either of us."

Crista nodded. "I'll ask Faron to help you. I've got the next watch on the bridge."

"Wait, if the AI is offline, then who has been assisting me with navigation?" Helna asked.

"The navigation computer, while it is the most advanced computer on the train, it's still only a sub-system of the AI. It can function without the AI being online." Janb replied.

"So, what are we missing because she is offline?" Crista asked.

"Well, once fully operational, she will be capable of controlling the engine during the night for us. She will also have the ability to monitor all our sensor systems as well as listen to the met reports and flare warnings," Janb replied. "She will also monitor the status of our cargo and passengers and let us know if there is a problem."

Crista just stared at her. "So didn't you think either Faron or I should have been told we were operating half blind?"

"Since neither of you had asked for her," Janb replied shrugging. "I didn't think you needed her yet. I was going to ask for your assistance at dinner."

"Okay girls, from now on, let either Faron or I know if anything happens or isn't working correctly. We need to know everything that's going on, even if you don't think it's going to affect anything. Do you understand?" Crista explained, trying to keep her anger at the mistake in check. "I'm sorry I upset you, Crista. I honestly didn't think it mattered," Janb said apologetically.

"I know that, B. That's why I'm not mad at you, but the situation. We should have made all this clear before we left port," Crista explained, using her pet name for Janb.

"I guess that's the reason I can't get into the flight navigation instruction," Helna said quietly.

"No, and what it means is that until the AI can resume her duties, you three will help Faron and I pull watch on the bridge, so we can monitor the weather and flare alert network. You will also monitor the comms traffic and keep an eye on the status boards for any malfunctions." When she saw the look on the girls' faces she explained.

"This isn't a punishment, girls. While the AI is offline, we have to do our best to cover for her. Just like we would for any other member of our team." She stood. "Now, Helna, it's your turn to cook tonight. Why don't you see if you can surprise Faron? I'm gonna go let him know the status of the AI, and see if he can help B get her fixed up."

When Crista told him of the mistake regarding the AI, Faron thoughtfully nodded his head. "Do you think a team spending time in a simulator would help correct problems like this?"

Crista considered his suggestion. "Probably. It would also serve to give the other teams time to adjust to each other."

"Are any of you unhappy with me?" Faron asked. "It's only been a couple of days."

"No!" Crista said quickly. "Not at all. You're everything we thought you'd be and more. I was thinking simulator time would be good for *other* teams, not ours. Compatibility is not an issue; communication is. I've already talked to the girls about it, and that should put an end to it."

"Okay, but I also want to tell them, probably over dinner, that if there is ever a problem between any of us to please talk about it. Personal issues can't be dealt with if no one knows of them," Faron replied. "As for the AI, I'll be glad to help Janb; I rated highest in engineering, but I wasn't too bad at programming either."

"It has occurred to me that this might be a ploy to get you alone for an hour or so. Just so you're aware this might be a setup," Crista suggested.

Faron grinned. "I don't mind at all. But, what I would like to know is alone time with me something all of you would like from time to time?"

"Well, we do love each other, but our relationship with you is still pretty new. Most of our experience has been with each other. So, yeah, I don't think the girls would mind randomly spending a night alone with you; I know I sure wouldn't, but until the AI is back online, we're going to have to wait. One of us should be available at all times."

Faron nodded. "I agree. I'll toss out the idea of one on one nights tonight at dinner."

"If you can, I would also suggest randomly 'surprising' each of the girls. That would make their year!"

"You and the girls were together in school right?" Faron asked.

Crista nodded. "Yeah, we did make that obvious didn't we?"

Faron grinned. "Yes, you did. What I was thinking was since you were the dominant one in the group; perhaps they would like a night alone with you as well."

"Possibly, you're the main attraction right now though," Crista said, smiling.

"Command, this is Gracen. May I ask what's going on up there?"

Since Faron was busy, Crista replied. "That would require a bit of an explanation Elder. The short version is we are chasing a very unusual level four plus sand storm to discover why it's not acting normally. It does have the potential to do serious damage to Cerberus, and any other facility in its path."

"Have you informed Elder Bollum?" Gracen asked.

"No Ma'am. We lost all contact due to the composition of the sand in this area," Crista replied.

"Lowering ride height to seven meters, stabilizers to maximum," Faron could be heard saying in the background.

"I understand why you're doing it, but what is the danger to us?" Gracen replied.

Crista was closely monitoring Faron, so she seemed a little distracted. "According to the information given to us by the engineers, through Elder Bollum, this level of storm should be nothing more than a minor irritation to us."

"Captain, ground object avoidance sensors are all but blind due to the metamaterial in the sand. At our current speed, I recommend returning us to a ride height of teen meters or possibly more," the AI suggested.

"Understood Artemus, returning to ten-meter ride height, please keep an eye on the wind speed," Faron replied as he raised the train back to ten meters.

The height difference was felt immediately as the wind slammed into the side of the fast-moving train. The stabilizers did their job well though and held the train steady.

"Current wind velocity is two hundred ninety to three hundred twenty klicks. Category five is confirmed, and the storm is continuing to increase in strength. I anticipate cat-six strength before we reach the core," Artemus informed them.

"Artemus, prepare to take the controls," Faron replied.

"I have control, Captain. You can release the controls now," the AI said. The Pilot's chair released Faron and he removed his goggles.

"Elder Gracen, this is Faron. Elder Bollum implied that we need to look into events like this storm. It was the main reason this entire train was built. I'm sorry if our actions have frightened you, but we need to investigate this."

"I understand, Captain. I was asked to consult on the received transmissions as well. I don't think any of us believed they would get here this quickly, though," Gracen replied.

"Yeah, In all honesty, I feel this is probably nothing more than a fluke weather system. It will serve as a good practice for us though. If it isn't, then we will have discovered the threat to our home much sooner than anticipated," Faron explained.

"You are correct, of course. If you would, could you let me see the data you have and are currently gathering? I'm not a meteorologist, but I might be able to help."

"Certainly, Elder! Artemus, please share all our data with Elder Gracen, and leave her comm open to the bridge," Faron ordered.

"Of course, Captain," the AI replied.

"One question, if I may, Captain?" Gracen asked. "Why have you not engaged the stealth systems?"

"Ah, because of the storm, Elder. Currently, the storm is concealing us, however, because of the static generated by the blowing sand, not only would it waste energy, but it would also make us more visible to external sensors," Jana answered for Faron.

"Okay, that makes sense," Gracen replied. "Thanks for indulging an old woman."

"Just because you are an Elder, does not make you old, Ma'am," Faron replied. "Besides, the bodies we're in don't actually age do they?"

"No, they do not. Which is how an old woman like me can still appear to look young and attractive," Gracen replied coyly.

"I would disagree with you, Elder, however, this is neither the time nor the place for that. While we have been hardened against most severe storms, we still need to stay focused on the task at hand," Faron said.

"Of course, Captain," Gracen replied. She sounded amused and not upset.

"Artemus, when we enter the eye, reduce speed to point five, engage all stealth systems, and do a full scan; orbital as well, if possible," Faron ordered. "I'd like to know if there's anything above this."

"Storm has reached category six in strength. Low altitude static discharge is becoming more prevalent," Artemus reported. "Winds are out of the south at three hundred fifty to three hundred ninety. We will enter the core in ten minutes."

"Thank you, Artemus. Steady as she goes," Faron replied.

"Captain, external temperatures are dropping rapidly, and barometric pressure is continuing to drop as well," Artemus reported. "Although I would expect this as we get near the eye, this is far too much of a drop for a normal storm. I recommend extreme caution, Captain."

"Janb, weapons status?" Faron asked.

"All weapons are on warm standby, shields are at maximum," Janb replied.

"Using passive scanners only, begin searching for targets," Faron ordered. "Artemus, reduce our speed and ride height as far as you can and still hold her steady, please."

"Reducing speed to one-point-two, ride height now seven," Artemus replied. "Great Wall Mountains four-hundred-twenty klicks present course."

"Understood, Artemus. I plan on turning long before we get there," Faron replied.

Suddenly, as if leaving one room for another, the weather outside the train cleared. "Captain we are in the eye. Speed reducing to point-nine, ride height five. Stealth systems are active," Artemus reported.

"Still no comms, Faron, not even nav beacons," Crista reported.

"Be sure we're recording everything we can, I'm sure someone would like to know all about this," Faron said.

"Contact! I have a target, Captain!" Janb said excitedly.

"What and where B?" Faron asked.

"Almost directly above us, distance twelve hundred. I can't tell what kind of beam it's firing, but it's not focused on the ground; it's like a cone disbursing energy," Janb replied.

"Captain, destroy it!" Gracen replied. "It's causing this storm, on my authority, I am ordering you to destroy that thing."

Faron sighed. "Janb, go active and bring it down. Try to get as much information on it as you can before it breaks up."

"Uh, yes sir," Janb replied. "Target locked. It appears to be an unmanned satellite, firing! Tracking... Target destroyed."

Faron nodded. "Good job, please return to passive scanning, but leave the weapons active. Artemus, how close to the center of the eye are we?"

"I have been circling it, Captain," the AI reported.

"For now keep us here. Reduce speed if you have to; we need to make sure this storm is dissipating," Faron ordered.

"Understood, Captain. Temperature and Barometric pressure seem to have stabilized, and the wind speed at the edge of the eye has begun to drop. The low-pressure cell above us is rapidly shrinking," Artemus replied. "I would conclude this storm had been artificially created by the unknown satellite for, as yet, unknown reasons."

"I think we know the damn reasons! This was an attack!" Gracen replied angrily.

"Forgive me Elder, but I don't think so," Crista replied as gently as she could. "Ma'am, with respect, if this was an attack, it was a poorly planned one. Seriously, what was the target? Cerberus? This wasn't even close to the strength needed to damage that facility. It simply doesn't make sense."

"Not taken by itself, no, it doesn't make sense. But perhaps there is information we are currently unaware of," Faron said thoughtfully. "Either way, this storm is over, and very soon we can resume our mission."

"Captain, the eye is collapsing, I recommend retracting the weapons to avoid damage to them," Atremus said.

Faron nodded to Janb who was looking at him after that comment. The girl typed on her keyboard and said, "Weapons retracted and set to warm standby."

"Helna, reset the course for Cerberus. As soon as we can verify the beacon, we'll get moving again," Faron replied.

Crista was watching the storm on the radar as well as through external cameras. "Wow, it's like someone shut off a switch."

Faron chuckled. "Well, we kinda did." He paused. "Elder Gracen, are you well?"

"Yes, I am, thank you, Captain. Also, thank you XO for the wake-up. The received signals scared a lot of us. I guess I let my emotions get the better of me when you detected that satellite. Thank you for correcting me," Gracen replied.

Seeing the storm was indeed dissipating, Faron spoke to Artemus. "Do we know our location, Artemus?"

"Yes, Captain."

"Do we have a course to Cerberus?" Faron asked.

"Yes Captain, however, we still do not have the beacon. Enough sand remains in the air to distort that signal," Artemus replied.

"Set ride height ten and ahead medium for Cerberus pass. Continue to monitor the dissipation of the storm, and alert me as soon as we reestablish communications. I need to make a report to Elder Bollum. Good work everyone," Faron replied and rose to get a drink from the machine. "Anyone else want something?"

They had no sooner gotten moving than they detected the Cerberus beacon but still had not yet gotten communications with the rest of the world. The beacon contact was intermittent, but clearing as the massive storm dissipated.

"Captain, we are receiving a priority hail from Cerberus Station," Artemus reported.

"Don't mention the contact or destroying the satellite. We'd like to avoid public panic for the time being. The Elders will release a statement as soon as we investigate this more," Gracen ordered.

"Yes, Ma'am. I had assumed that was classified since our real mission is also classified," Faron replied. "Artemus, let's say hi to Cerberus again."

"Comm open, Sir."

"Cerberus control, this is one-niner-three super heavy. Did ya miss us?" Faron asked.

"Yes, we did actually. Your arrival is overdue, we were afraid you fell victim to the storm," the controller replied.

"After we lost contact with you, and since we are armored against storms, we decided to head for the eye of the storm to try to gather more information for the weather folks to look over. However, by the time we got there, the system had already started dissipating.

"I know the unannounced deviation is against the rules Control, however, we do have a special mandate given us by Elder Bollum to investigate things of this nature. I am sorry if we worried you," Faron replied.

"Damn, and here I was getting ready to chew you out for breaking the rules on your first run," a more senior-sounding voice replied, sounding slightly amused.

"I am sorry, sir. Perhaps I can think of something minor to screw up, the next time we come through," Faron replied grinning.

"I'll forgive you if you can slow down enough for us to get a good look at ya. We've never heard of a storm-proof train before," Control said.

"I think that can be arranged, Control." Faron checked his console. "We should be over your outer marker in about forty-five minutes at present speed."

"Confirmed, one-niner-three. We'll see you then. Thanks for not being dead."

"It's our pleasure, control. One-niner-three, out." Faron closed the comm.

"Sir, Elder Bollum is on the comm for you also. He would like to speak to you and Elder Gracen in private," Artemus said.

Faron nodded as he stood. "Crista, you have command."

The girl winked at him as she moved over to his, now empty, chair.

Faron engaged the privacy screen in the alcove off the bridge for private communications. When he did the hologram of the waiting call came up in the table. An image of Elder Bollum and Elder Gracen was displayed.

"Elders, how may I be of service?" Faron asked politely.

"Well, first off, you can quit scaring the hell out of your passengers!" Gracen said. She was grinning so he knew she was teasing him. Bollum just chuckled.

"We lost all of your data feeds, so I was contacting you for an explanation." Elder Bollum held up a hand. "We've been receiving all the data you gathered, but I wanted your personal opinion."

"Make sure it's classified, Bollum. This was *not* a normal storm," Gracen replied.

"Oh?" Bollum asked as he could be seen to type on something unseen. "In what way?"

"You tell him, Captain. I'm still trying to come to terms with this," Gracen replied seriously.

Faron nodded. "Sir, this 'storm' was nothing of the sort. It was an attack seemingly against the Cerberus facility. The weather event was being artificially created by an object in a very low orbit. After gathering as much data as possible, we shot the object down, ending the 'event'.

"Sir, you told us you were worried about the ancestors on Earth coming for us; I'd say they are most likely here already," Faron replied.

Gracen looked at Faron in surprise and fear. "How did you arrive at that conclusion based on a single encounter with an unmanned 'probe'?"

"With respect Elder, it would make no sense at all to send an isolated and unmanned craft here, simply to test the viability of using weather as a weapon. No, there has to be another, manned craft, somewhere in our system, or on the planet," Faron reported. "That's the only way what we saw would make any sense at all, sir."

"Have you discussed this with your crew, Faron?" Bollum asked.

"Sir, I haven't even discussed it with Elder Gracen. No, unless they reached this conclusion on their own, They know nothing of my assumptions," Faron replied. "This changes almost everything, doesn't it, Sir?"

"Yes, it does, son, rather drastically." He cleared his throat. "Captain. You are to dock at Cerberus and refill the fuel cells depleted in the latest... 'storm'. Once complete, proceed through the pass, but return to base via the Deep Sand entrance for restock and more passengers. When you get in here, be subtle; we will be increasing construction on the bays and it'll most likely be very crowded in here."

"Orders understood, Sir," Faron replied. "We are scheduled to pass through Cerberus in about thirty minutes, Sir. Please, excuse me for a moment." Bollum nodded as he opened a comm to the pilot.

"Crista, we need to resupply the fuel for Cerberus. Please adjust the course and obtain docking clearance at their fuel pods. I'll be up soon to fill you all in on the rest of the changes," Faron ordered.

"We're not going across the great desert anymore are we?" Crista asked.

"Not this trip. See ya in a few," Faron said and closed the comm.

He smiled at Elder Bollum. "Further orders, Sir?"

"No, just calling to get your take on the storm. I had no idea I was sending you folks out to be attacked on your first run," Bollum replied.

"Well, in all honestly, sir, this might not have been an attack. We have no idea what they were doing out there. As much as I hate to say it, until we start getting shot at, I don't think we're looking at attacks," Faron replied.

"What else could they be?" Gracen asked.

Faron shrugged. "Honestly, I have no idea. But the fact does remain that no one was hurt, nor could they have been. This could have been just about anything, but I would have a hard time believing that they came across the galaxy just to perform weather experiments." He was thoughtful for a moment. "I won't rule out the possibility they will try to contact us before they invade or attack. Has anyone simply tried to contact the ones in the system?"

"No, not yet. Frankly, I don't think the possibility has even occurred to them either," Bollum replied.

"If we can get them to talk, even if it's an argument, that's more time we have to get our defenses built," Faron replied.

"If you're not careful Son, you're going to end up back here in charge of all of this," Bollum replied grinning.

"The ladies would hunt both of us down, Sir!" Faron replied.

"Captain, we're approaching Cerberus Fuel Depot," Crista called.

Faron nodded. "On my way, Crista." He looked back at the Elders. "Please excuse me, Elders; duty calls."

"We'll visit more when you get back here, Captain. Safe Journey," Bollum said, dismissing him.

Faron smiled at Elder Gracen. "Ma'am, I've been asked to invite you to dinner tonight." \

"It would be my honor, Captain. Thank you," Elder Gracen replied. Faron turned the display off before opening the privacy field and heading for his pilot's chair.

"New orders, Faron?" Helna asked.

Faron nodded. "Yep, I'll fill you guys in on them while the outpost fuel cells are being refilled."

"Cerberus station, this is one-niner-three super heavy. I understand you folks might need some gas?" Faron called.

"Now that's damn fast service! I only put in the request for that a few minutes ago!" the older-sounding voice replied.

"We live to serve, Sir. Reducing speed to five hundred, distance is one-five-zero," Faron replied.

"On the path, Super Heavy." The controller replied once again. "You know, we have to come up with a good name for you; Super Heavy is too boring!"

Faron grinned. "Ask control to alter our ID to Sand Raptor one-niner-three."

"Alteration is approved," Artemis reported. "IFF ID now changed to Sand Raptor One-Niner-Three.

"Now *that* was fast!" Crista replied.

"Creepy-fast!" Cerberus replied. "Do you have an Elder riding with you or something?"

"Cerberus, you know better than to ask such things!" Faron replied. "Their movements are never announced."

"There is no way you went storm chasing with an Elder on board!" Cerberus replied.

"Then you answered your own question, didn't you? Speed now one hundred, distance fifty. I have a visual on the depot," Faron reported. "Stand by for docking and fuel transfer. JanA, JanB, please go back to the fuel cars and assist in the unloading." He made sure the comm was off. "I'm only asking so you can make sure those yokels don't blow us all up."

Both girls giggled and kissed his cheeks as they ran for the exit.

"Holy... Just how big are you?" the older man could be heard again. "Sand Raptor, be advised that, the docking port will be at maximum extension to reach your portal once you align with the fuel depot." He was quiet for a moment. "We've never had to worry about a train connecting to both areas before now."

"Understood, Cerberus. I'll make a note in my log suggesting your docking port be remodeled to accommodate the larger trains," Faron replied. "Also, you might want to send a VIP protocol to the docking area."

"I thought you said you didn't have an Elder with you?" the operator said.

"No," Faron replied. "I said their movements are not announced, however, arrivals usually are." He paused. "Docking will be complete in five minutes."

Looking through the optics of the docking area, Faron saw that it was full of people trying to see the new train. Briefly, he wondered if anyone was there to greet the Elder.

"Elder Gracen, we are docked to Cerberus Station. Departure will be in four hours if you would like to disembark. Per regulations, I did notify Cerberus control you were here," Faron said over the intercom.

"Thank you, Captain. I don't believe I need to leave the train at this point," Gracen replied.

Faron chuckled. "Probably a good thing, Elder. I believe the docking bay is full of people staring at the train."

"I can't blame them. We are something they have never seen before. That being said, I would think they would have duties they should be attending to," Elder Gracen replied, haughtily.

Quietly Helna said. "People *do* get down-time."

"Relax Helna, she was being sarcastic," Crista replied just as quietly.

"Besides Helna, we are expected to ask like this; it keeps people's animosity focused on us instead of each other," Gracen replied, making the girl realize she'd been overheard.

"Madam Elder," Faron began as he finished up the docking. "If I may ask, why do the Elders not only foster but ensure such anger is directed at them?"

"I'm only telling you this because there is a good chance one of you will be an Elder yourselves someday," Gracen paused as if to gather her thoughts. "We do not have a very large population as societies go. When we left Earth, the planetary population was nearing twenty billion. Violent crime was rampant; especially in or near the larger cities.

"Some psych, somewhere, observed that in areas that the population was focused on the leadership, there was not only less crime against the individual, there was actually less crime overall." She paused. "Now, we are not even close to that size, population-wise, and we have a much larger planet to spread out on, we still try to keep any and all negative feelings focused on us instead of other citizens. It sets a precedent that we hope will carry through to the future."

Faron nodded. "Keep people mad at their leadership and they won't be mad at each other?"

"It doesn't completely eliminate interpersonal conflict, but it has greatly reduced it," Gracen replied.

"I wonder what Earth's like now?" Helna asked rhetorically.

"It's either dying or already dead," Gracen replied. "They murdered it. I'll tell you folks all about it over dinner tonight, Okay?"

"Docking complete. Ride height anchored at five meters. Shielding merged with base; grounding complete. Fuel transfer is enabled," Faron said. "Artemus, we are standing down for three hours, forty-five minutes."

"We are stable and locked down, Captain," Artemus replied.

"Jan-twins; we are ready for the transfer," Faron said over the comm.

"Thanks! We'll get started as soon as we can get the suits on!" JanB replied.

"So, Elder Gracen, care to explain what's so wrong with the twins that it requires the designer of the simulant system to ride along on their maiden voyage?" Faron asked.

The hologram of the Elder narrowed her eyes at Faron. "How did you figure it out?"

Helna and Crista both gasped and stared at Faron like he was insane.

Faron shrugged. "Little things mostly. You just confirmed it for me. I assume they're not dangerous, or Crista and I would have a lot more training."

Gracen nodded. "They are unique and very precious; you see the host body of 'Jana' died in hibernation, twenty years ago. They do not have a host body like the rest of you, and exist completely in the bodies they have now."

"Wait, they had only one host, not two?" Helna asked. "I thought they were twins?"

"When we lost Jana in hibernation, the body she was riding also ceased function. So, to save one of them, we downloaded Jana into a new body while we tried to fix her biological one.

"We could not save her biological body, and her synthetic was mostly catatonic, we tried copying her data from the new synthetic into the old one. We got two different individuals that shared some data as well as some memories. *How* they are sharing is a question we still can't answer since they no longer have a functioning biological body." Gracen finished.

"My apologies, Elder. If Jana passed away, why did you allow the synthetics to live? What is the point?" Crista asked. Her voice was flat and neutral, almost hostile.

"Jana was an Elder and a member of the original colonists," Gracen replied. "Does this change how you feel about them, Crista?"

Crista shook her head. "No, I still love them. However, it does change my opinion of the Elders."

Gracen nodded her head. "Understandable. If it helps, you are not alone in your opinion, even among other Elders. When Jana died, her best friend and our resident sentient Artificial Intelligence followed her best friend into the dark. That left us with a standard artificial intelligent computer system called Sistern. It has all Bethany's knowledge, but none of her personality or what made her unique.

"It is hoped, at least by the scientific community, that the Jana synthetics will somehow remember how to create a sentient AI."

"With respect, Elder Gracen, the person you knew as Jana is no longer with us, and she will not be coming back," Crista said quietly. "However, *our* two wives might very well figure out how to do what you want."

"When are you going to tell them?" Faron asked.

Elder Gracen looked confused. "Tell who, what?"

"The twins; when are you going to tell them?" Faron asked.

"There are no current plans to inform them of their altered reality. It was decided to let them believe they are as human as the rest of us," Gracen replied.

"Excuse me, Elder, but they are already far more human than *you* are," Helna replied as she left the room in tears.

Crista kissed Faron before running after her.

"Perhaps it wasn't the wisest course of action to allow you to discover the truth," Gracen replied.

"Elder, some things must be allowed to come out slowly and with care. No one has the right to determine who can know what truths. The Girls need to be told the truth of their existence and the history of the woman that is a part of them," Faron replied. "In light of the current situation, perhaps we should postpone dinner this evening."

Gracen nodded sadly. "I fear you are correct, Captain. It would seem I am no longer welcome in your home."

"I am having a problem understanding something though; if they are so precious to you, why did you let them out of the city?" Faron asked. "Elder Bollum himself said this was going to be dangerous. Why would you risk them?"

Gracen shrugged. "I was against it, of course. However, they weren't growing and developing anymore. We held them in the labs with us for almost twenty years, and they never matured past the pre-teen stage. Once we allowed them to attend classes with the rest of the girls, they began growing again.

"Some of us felt that had been enough to get them over the hump and that we should bring them back into the lab, but several others wanted to see how far 'life experience' would let them grow."

"So, you view them as little more than hyper-intelligent AI that are riding androids?" Faron asked. He tried very hard not to look away at that point. He didn't want the Elder to notice the two girls' entrance onto the bridge.

"Well, not so much, no. At least not any more than the rest of us are. I'd like to think this experiment means that even if we pass on, we can remain as long as our bodies continue to function," Gracen mused.

"I'm sorry to tell you this, Elder, but you're way off base there," Jana 'A' said. Beside her, her 'sister' nodded in agreement.

"Girls?" Gracen asked, completely surprised.

Continued in Episode two

Continued in Episode two

Don't miss out!

Visit the website below and you can sign up to receive emails whenever Ben Winston publishes a new book. There's no charge and no obligation.

https://books2read.com/r/B-A-LTP-HQPUC

BOOKS2READ

Connecting independent readers to independent writers.

Did you love *Addran IV*? Then you should read *Ascension*[1] by Ben Winston!

Ariel Janis was a normal college girl until she attended the reading of a will. She inherited much more than she bargained for as she discovers more and more about her new estate. Not only is she now one of the richest women in the United States, she learns she has inherited the legacy of being a Guardian to a Galactic Empire she's never heard of. Just as she thinks she gets a handle on that, she gets a visit from a very important, very special guest from way out of town.

Read more at bluespace-publications.com.

---

1. https://books2read.com/u/4NGkRN

2. https://books2read.com/u/4NGkRN

About the Author

Ben Winston (1965 - ?) was born in Iowa and grew up in Minnesota on the family dairy farm. Upon reaching adulthood, he joined the United States Army as a communications technician. Before getting out of the military, he decided to go to school for computer electronics.

Shortly after getting out of the military, and after getting a new job with an over-seas company, he was diagnosed with Crohn's Disease. A month after beginning the new job, he was laid off due to budget over-runs on the project he was hired for. Upon returning to the United States, he had difficulty maintaining employment because of the chronic illness.

He began writing as a form of stress release, from being home bound and not being able to work, and found he liked writing erotica. Ben wrote a trilogy called the Talosian Chronicles (Currently in rewrite to remove the graphic sex and finalized his vision of the story). The first book, Star Dancer, won awards and was nominated for many others by the online communities where it was posted.

Ben Winston returned to school for literature, after completion, he began writing professionally. Being an avid fan of science fiction he focused on this genre. He was, and still is, influenced and inspired by Gene Roddenberry, Anne McCaffery, David Weber, Isaac Asimov, and Ray Bradbury. Some of his favorite movies and TV shows are; Battlestar Galactica (both versions), Andromeda, Star Trek, Firefly, Star Wars, and many of the B-rated movies that were actually box-office bombs.

Read more at bluespace-publications.com.

About the Publisher

Currently, only Michael McClain and Ben Winston are published through Blue Space Publications. It was formed by those authors with the sole purpose of publishing their works.

We have recently added a new author by the name of Ian Williams to the family.